Little Look and Find®

MARVEL

GUARDIANS OF THE GALAXY

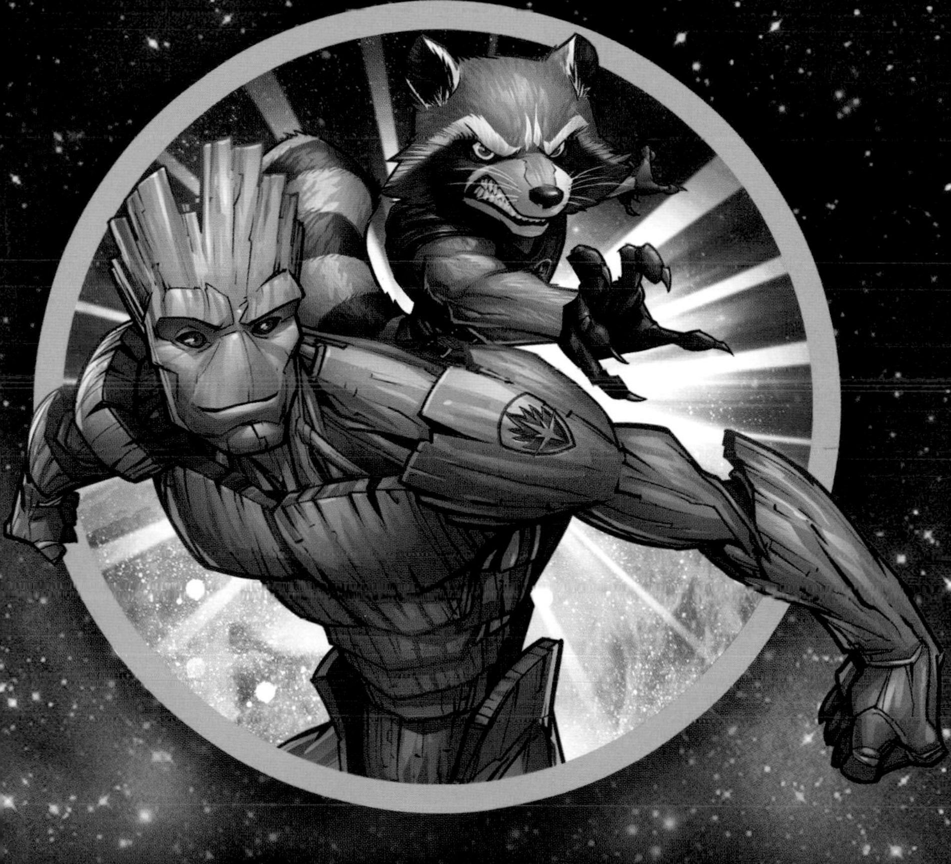

we make books come alive™

Phoenix International Publications, Inc.

Chicago • London • New York • Hamburg • Mexico City • Paris • Sydney

Peter Quill is in trouble! Thanks to a baggage mix-up at an interplanetary airport, a knapsack with his five favorite mix tapes has gone missing! Now, each tape has been flown to a different planet! Rocket Raccoon and his long-limbed pal, Groot, have promised to recover each of Peter's tapes. They start on Xandar, whose police forces are less than thrilled to see them.

While Rocket and Groot hunt for the first of Star-Lord's soundtracks, spot these Nova Corpsmen apprehending them:

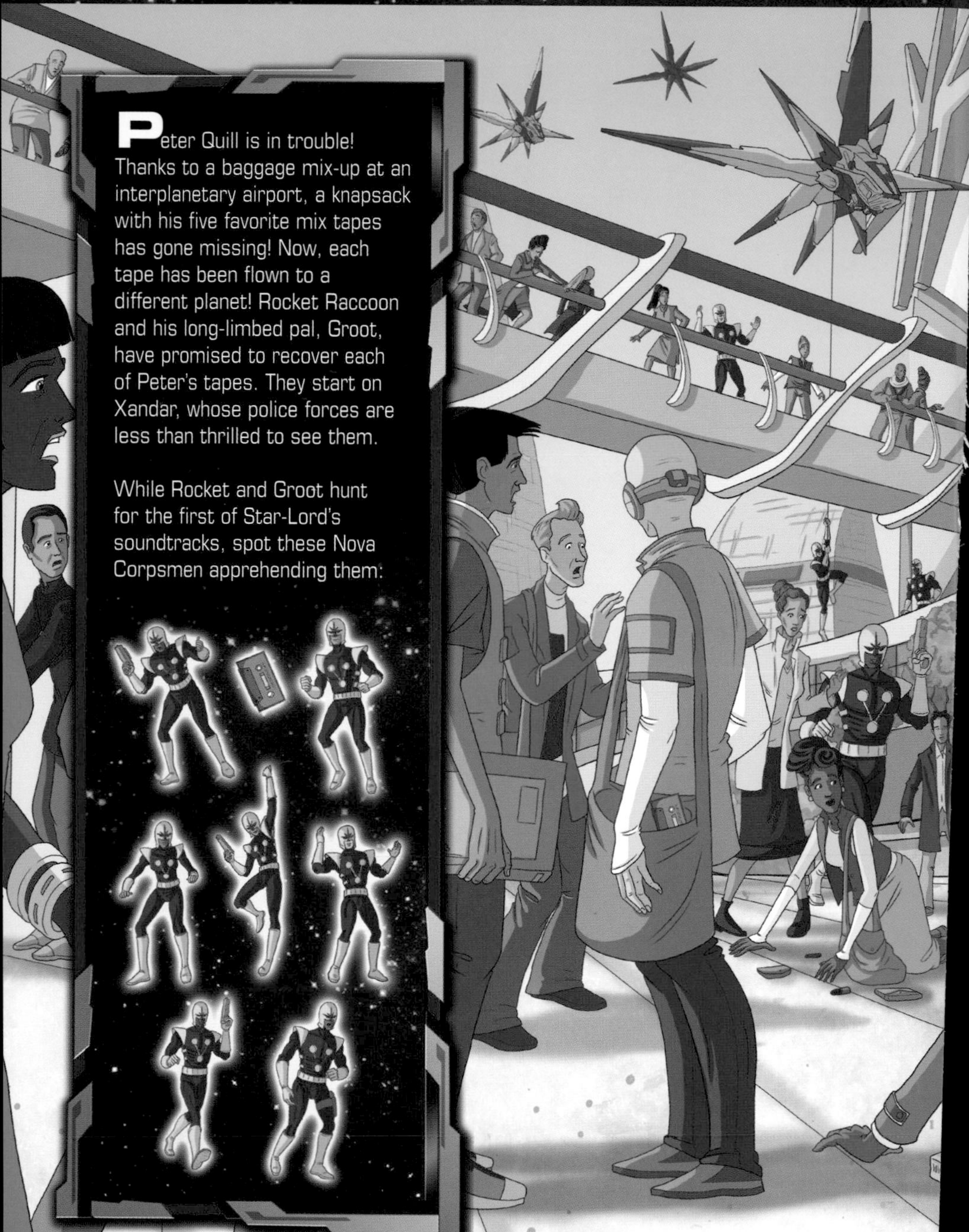

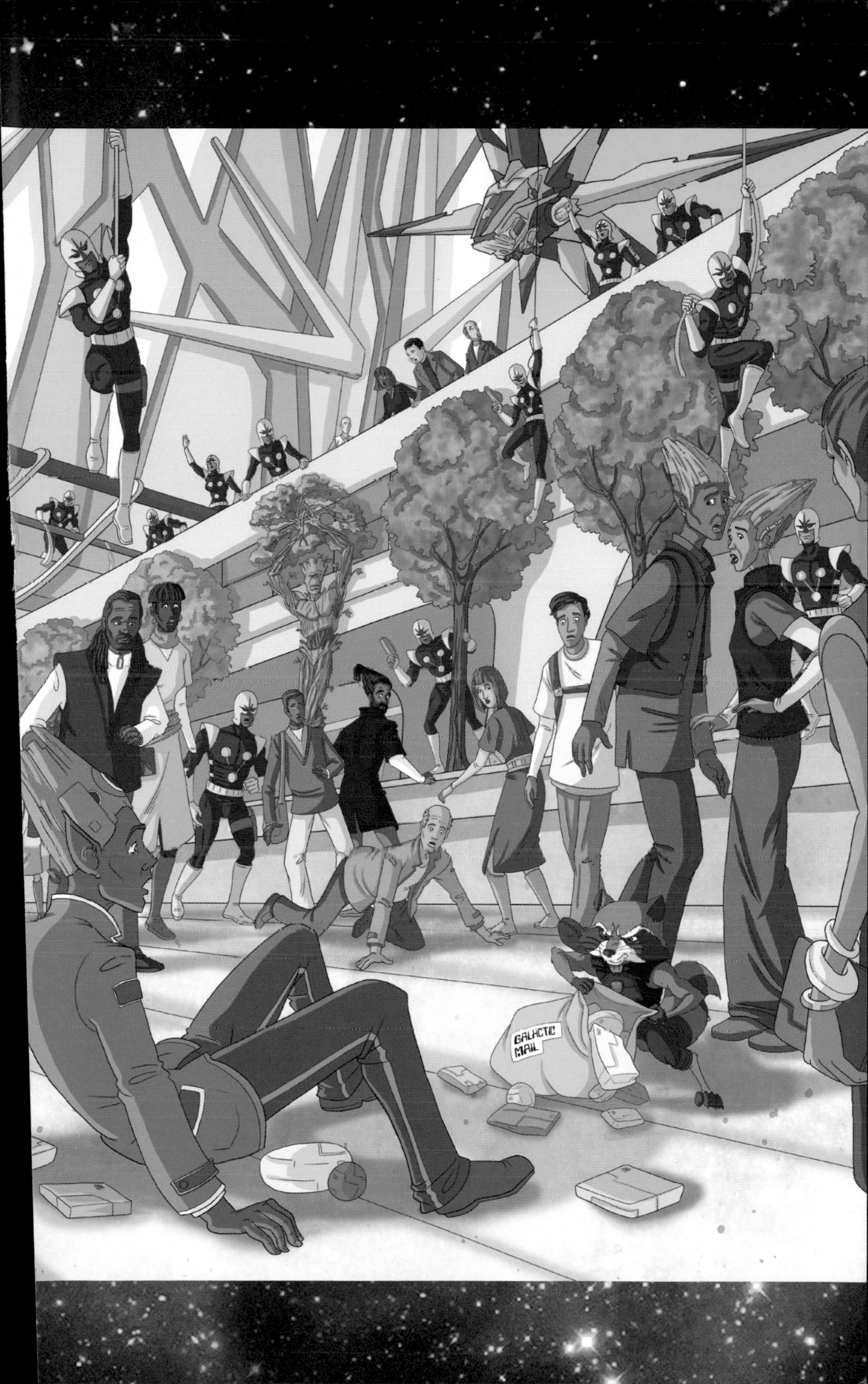
GALACTIC
MAIL

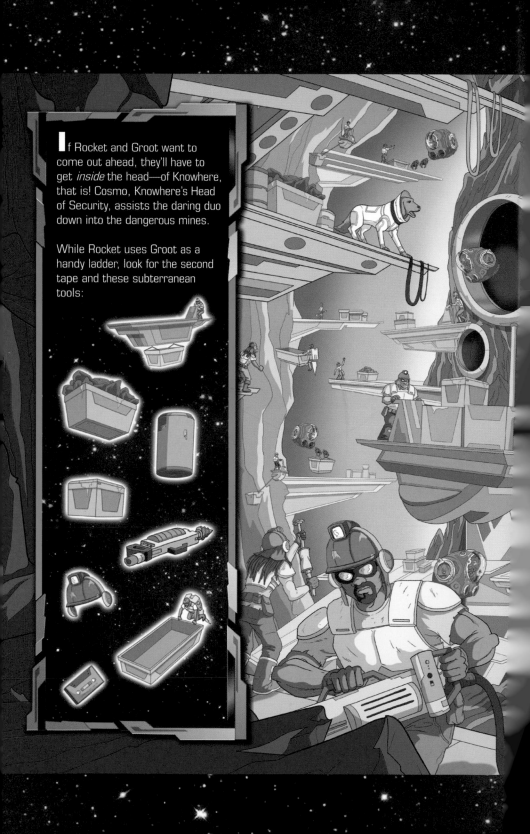

If Rocket and Groot want to come out ahead, they'll have to get *inside* the head—of Knowhere, that is! Cosmo, Knowhere's Head of Security, assists the daring duo down into the dangerous mines.

While Rocket uses Groot as a handy ladder, look for the second tape and these subterranean tools:

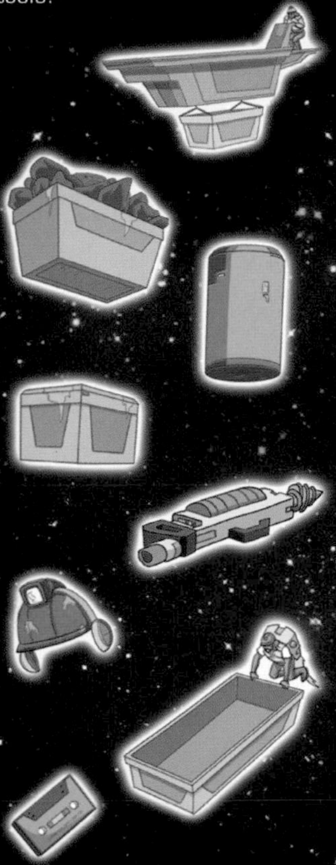

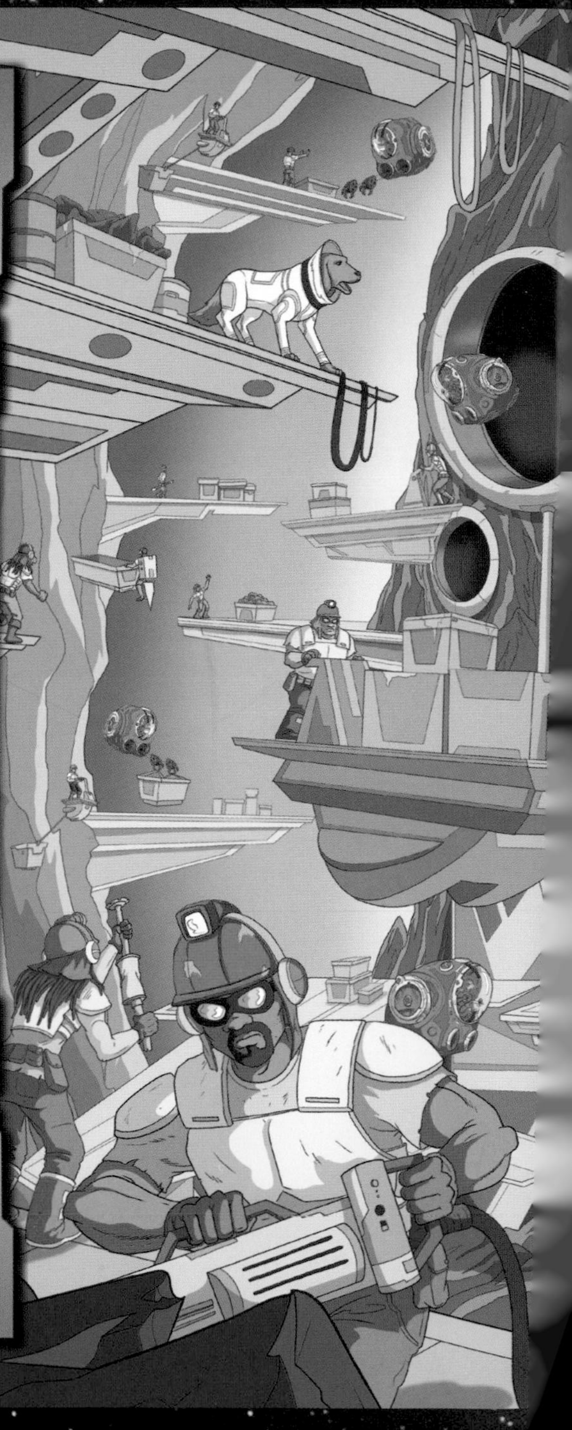

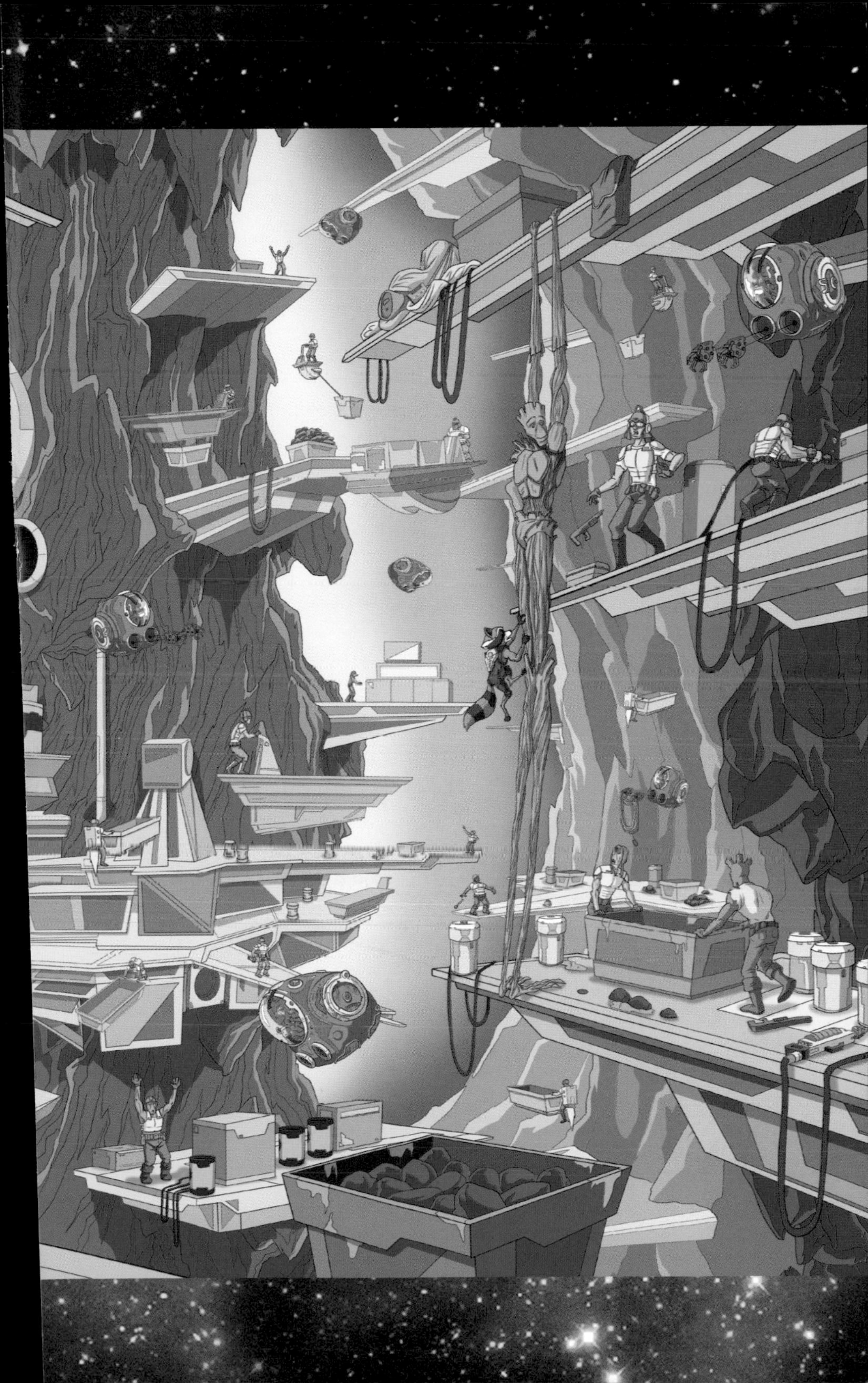

Groot and Rocket use Knowhere's Continuum Cortex to transport themselves to one of the strangest places ever: Planet Pinball! Designed to look like a beloved game from Peter Quill's home planet, this place is as fearsome as it is flashy.

While Rocket tries not to get flattened, track down the third tape along with these precarious pinball parts:

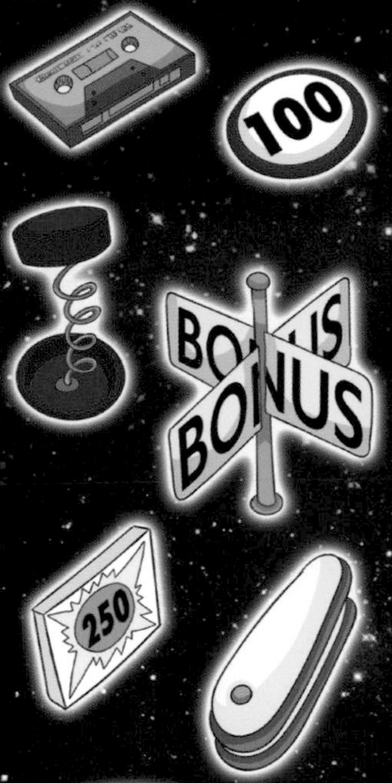

100
BONUS
BONUS
250

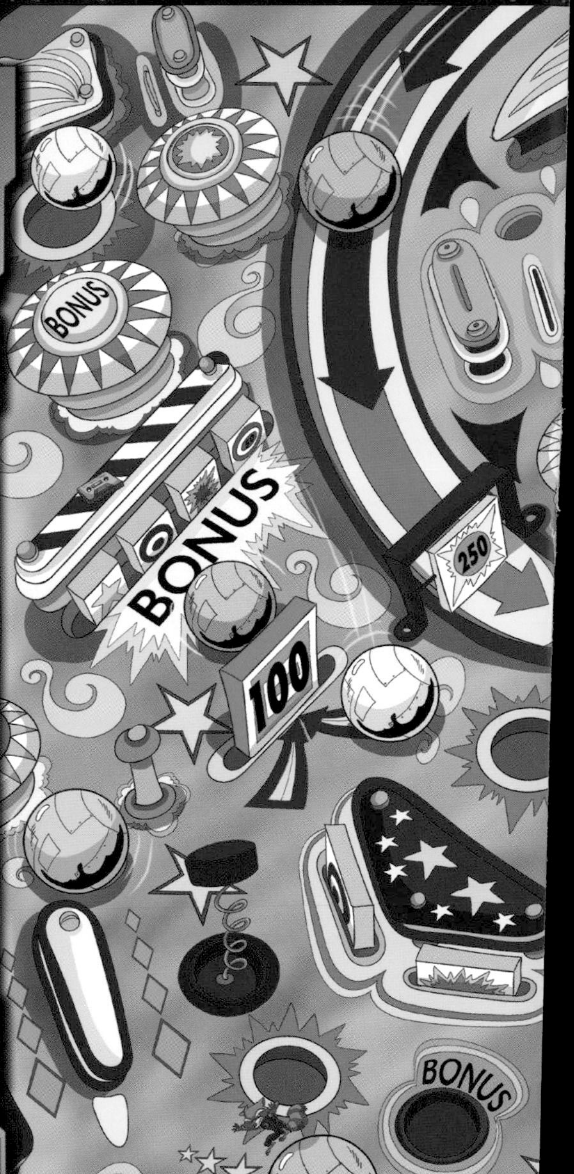

BONUS
BONUS
250
100
BONUS

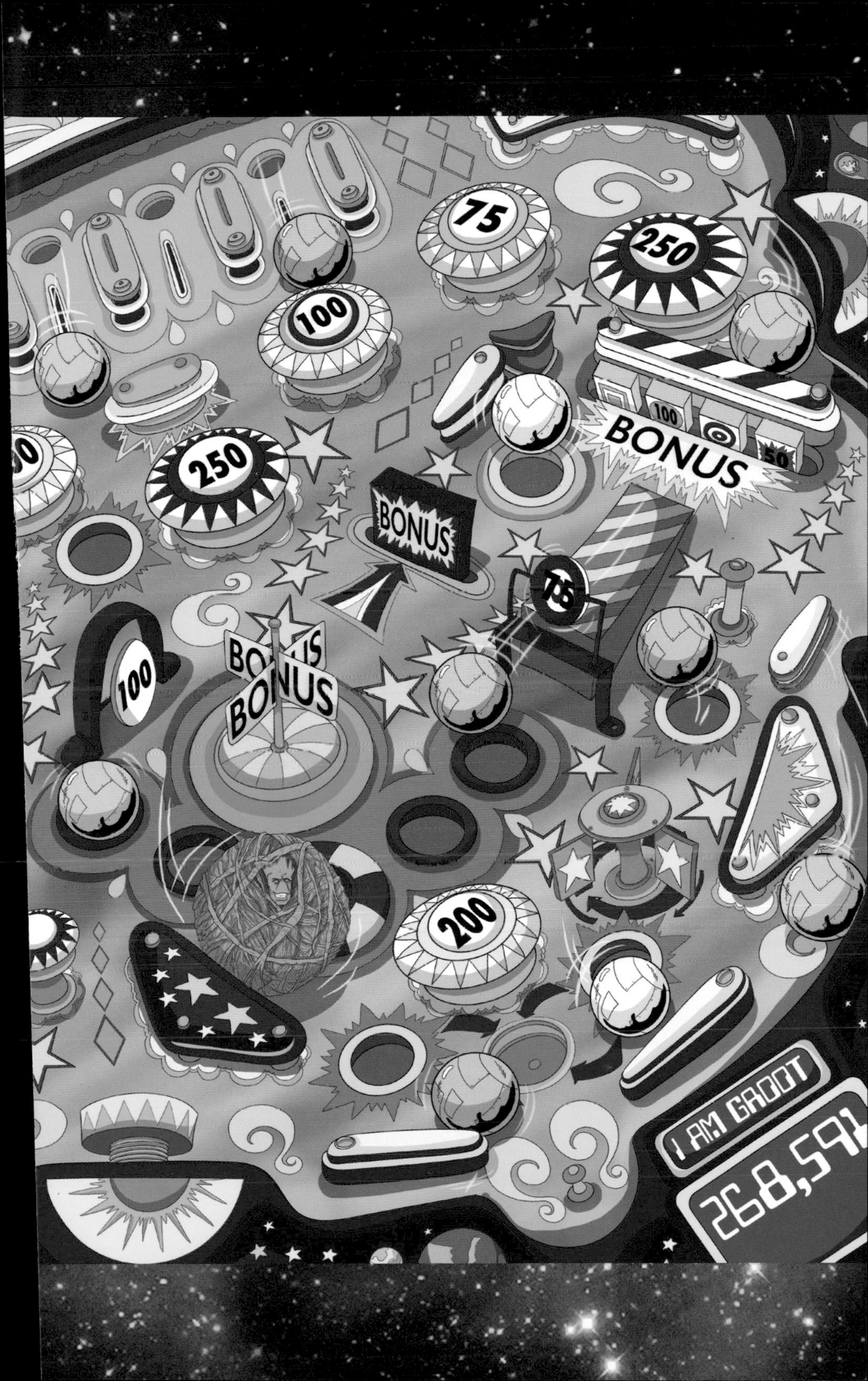
75
250
100
250
BONUS
100
50
BONUS
75
BONUS
BONUS
100
200
I AM GROOT
268,59

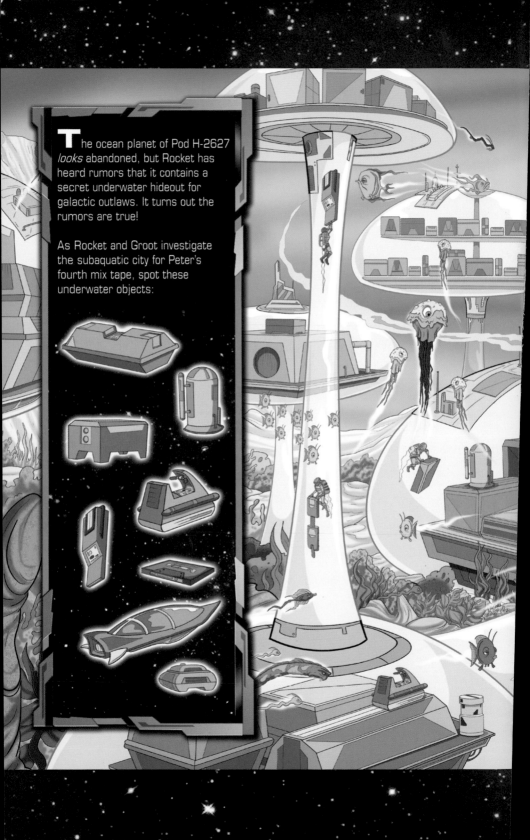

The ocean planet of Pod H-2627 *looks* abandoned, but Rocket has heard rumors that it contains a secret underwater hideout for galactic outlaws. It turns out the rumors are true!

As Rocket and Groot investigate the subaquatic city for Peter's fourth mix tape, spot these underwater objects:

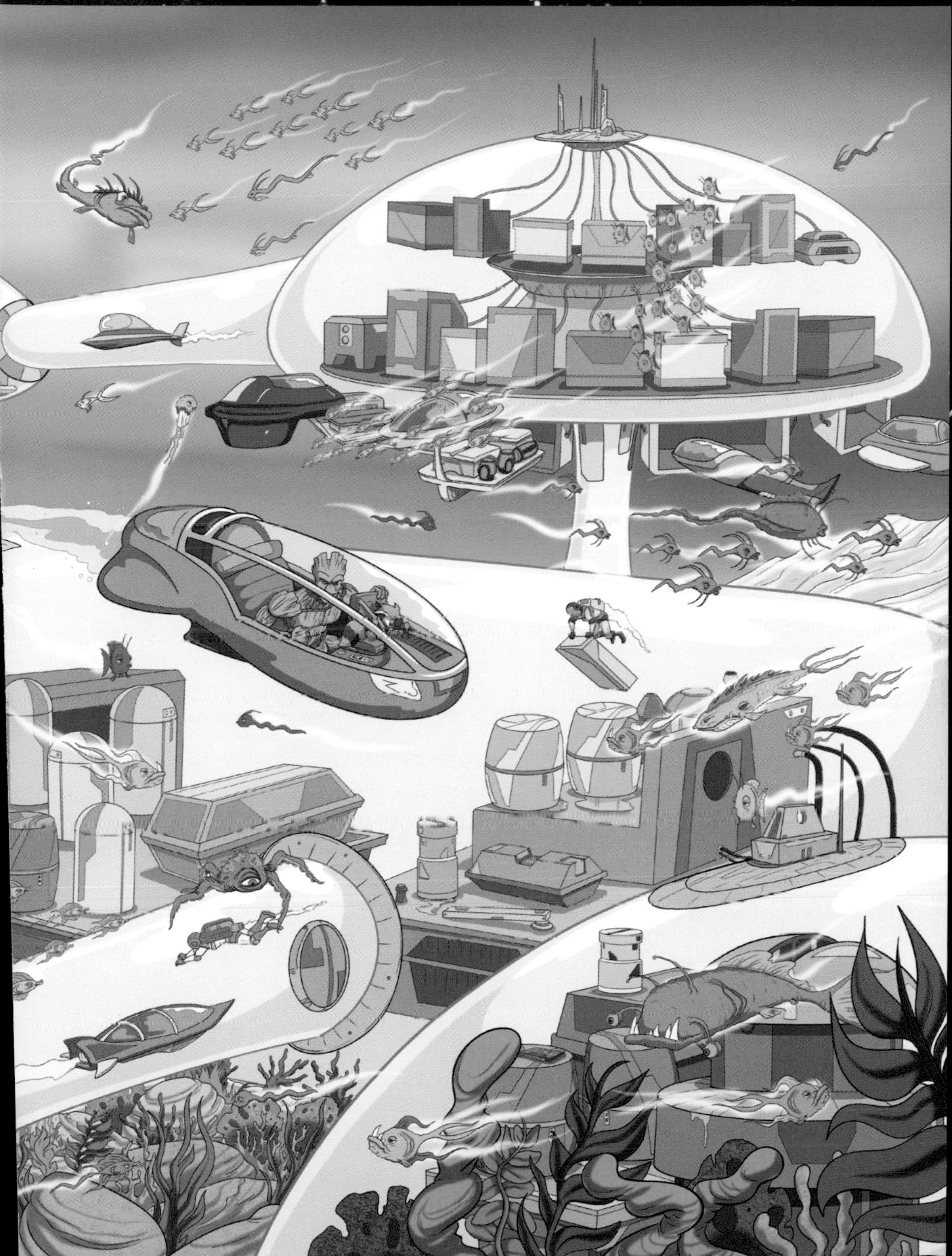

Next stop, Planet X—capital of the branch world and Groot's home planet! Groot was exiled from Planet X years ago, and his herbaceous brothers won't let him forget it.

As the panicked pair hightails it back to Rocket's ship, find the fifth tape as well as these Groot lookalikes:

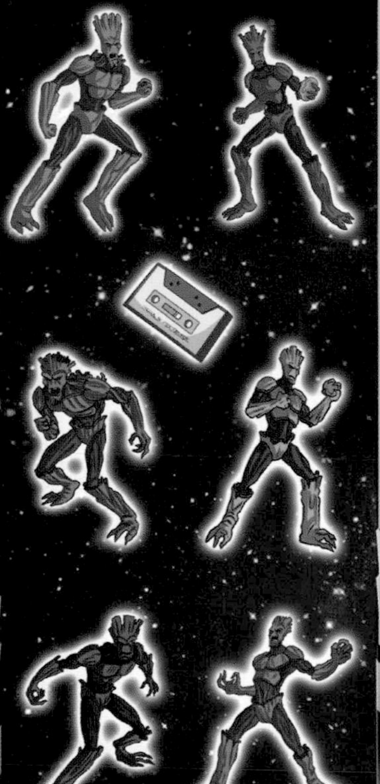

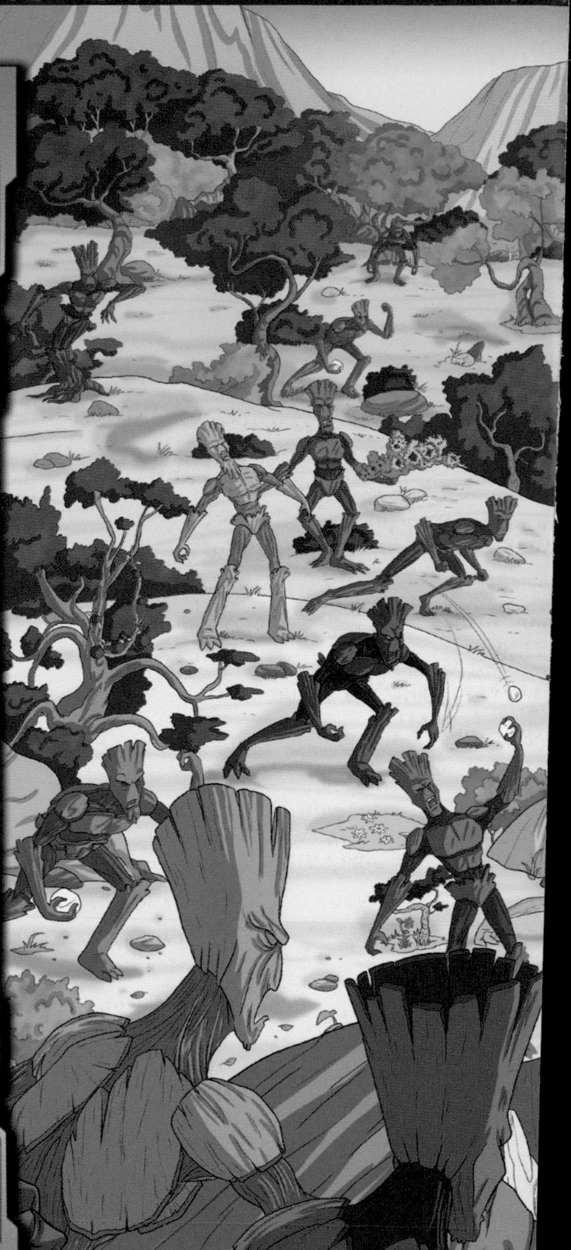

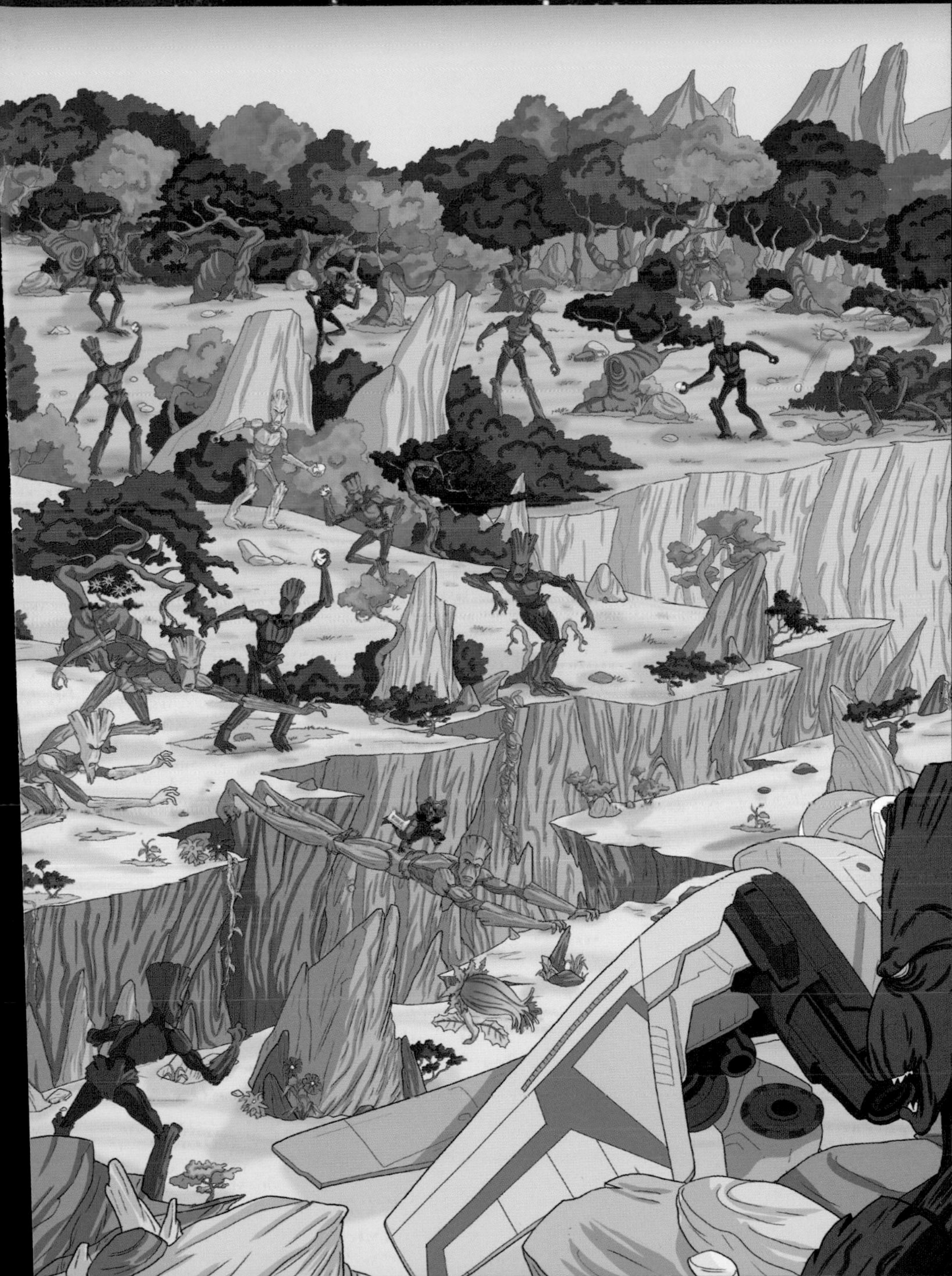

Rocket and Groot have snagged the last of Peter's mix tapes—but not before Groot was splintered to bits! Luckily, Rocket saved one of Groot's branches, and now Groot is safe by his side. Unfortunately, Yondu Udonta and his Ravagers have just picked up their signal, and they want to add Rocket's ship to their collection!

While Rocket tries to lose the Ravagers and return safely to Peter, spot these villainous vehicles:

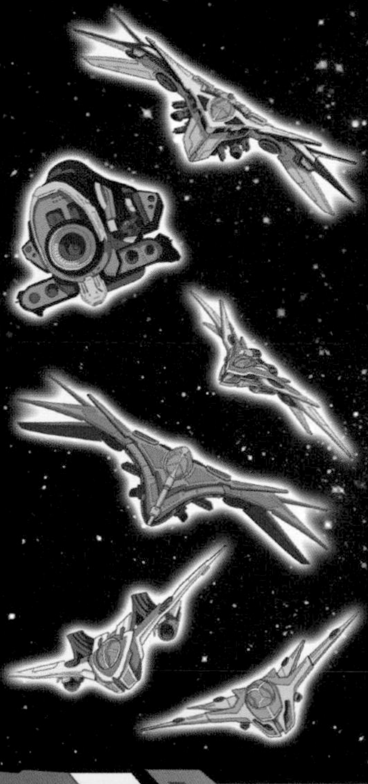

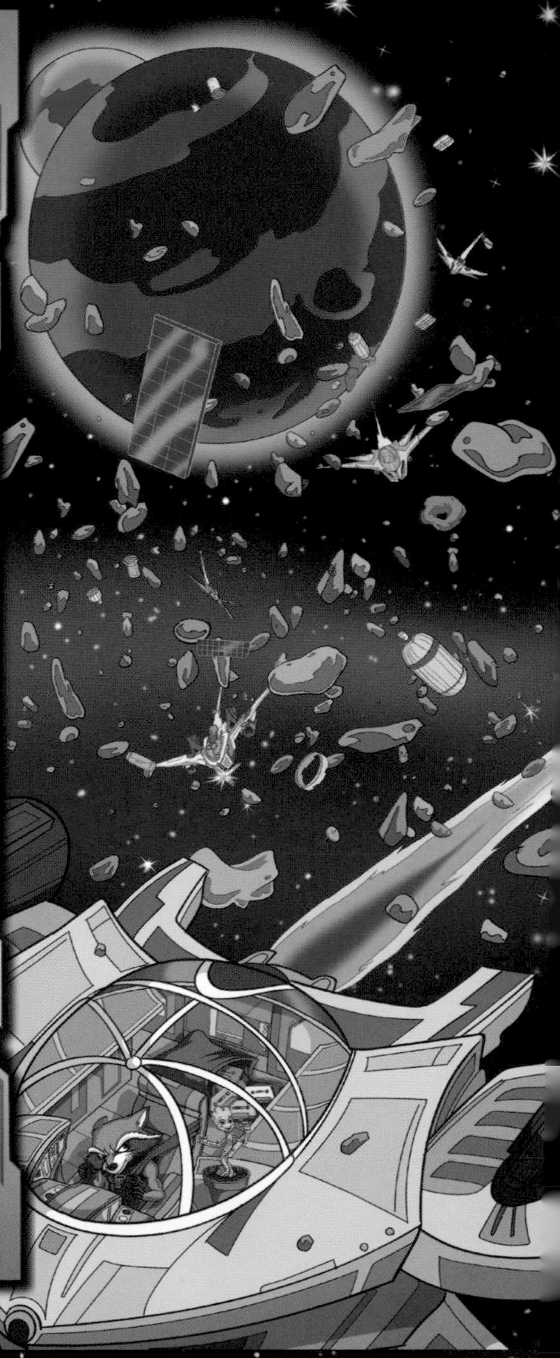

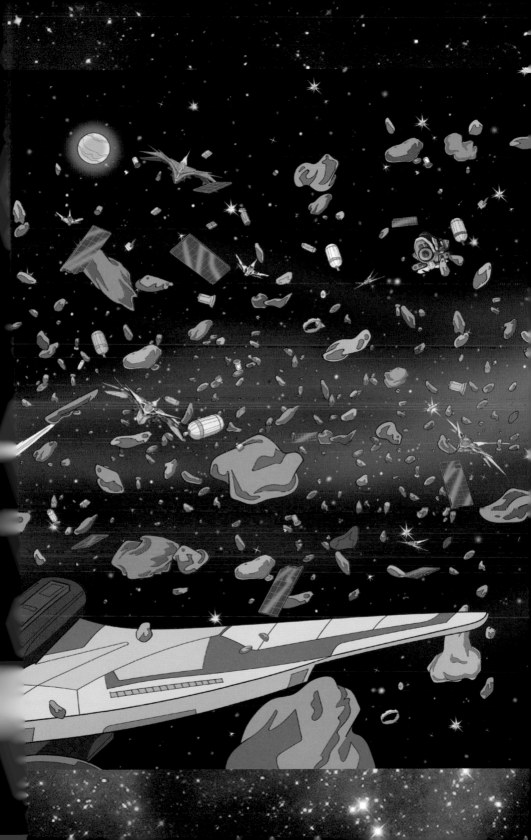

Just as the Ravagers close in, the *Milano* arrives to save the day! Star-Lord, Gamora, and Drax help Rocket and Groot fend off Yondu and his relentless Ravagers.

As the epic aerial battle ensues, point out these peculiar planets:

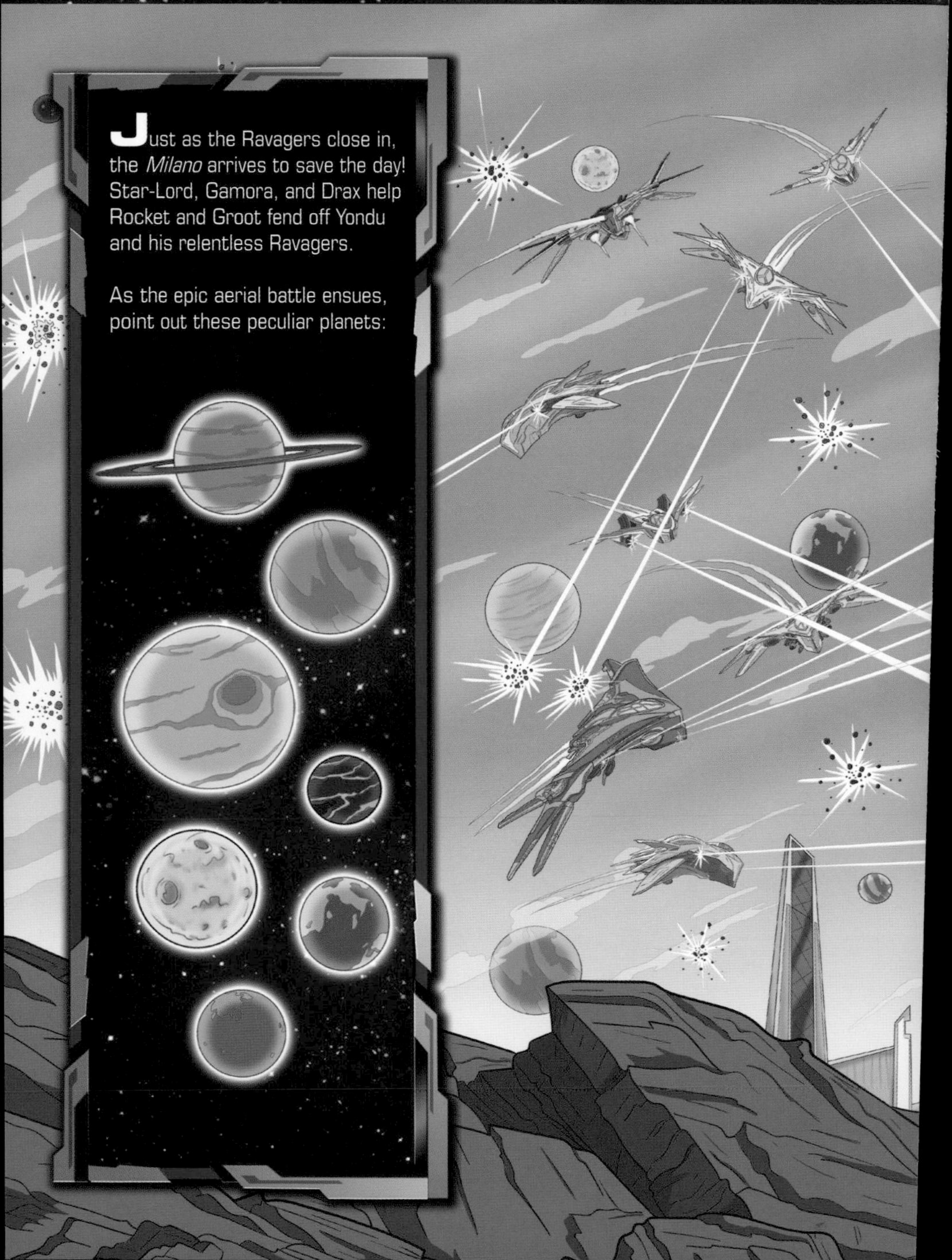

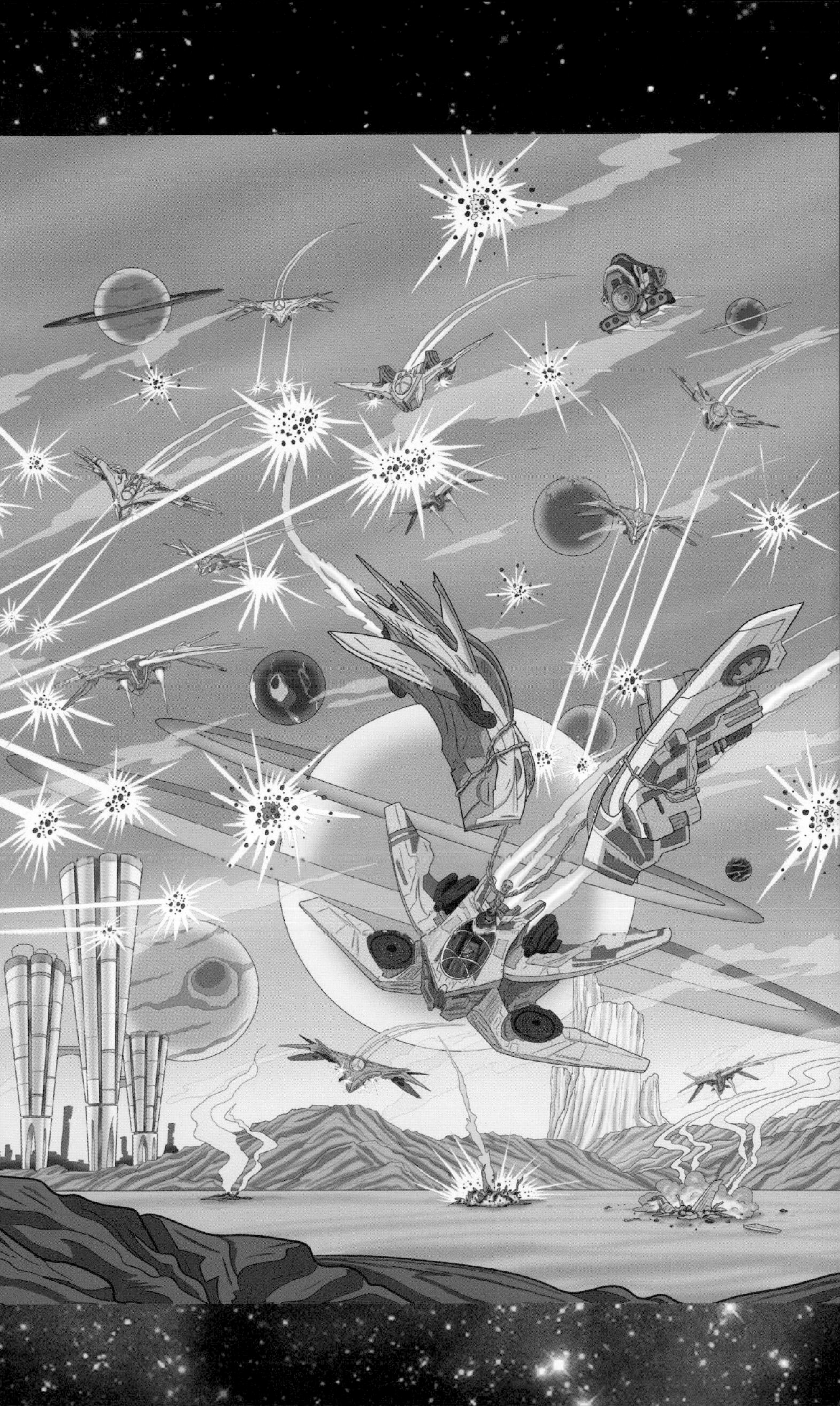

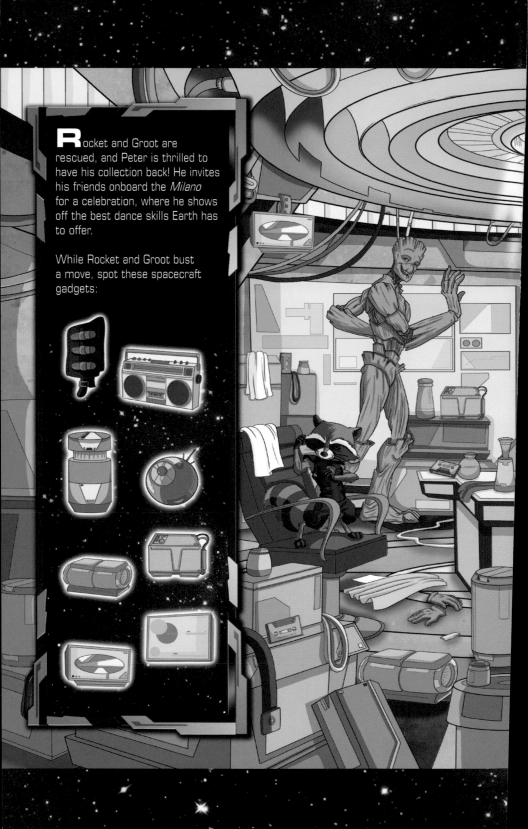

Rocket and Groot are rescued, and Peter is thrilled to have his collection back! He invites his friends onboard the *Milano* for a celebration, where he shows off the best dance skills Earth has to offer.

While Rocket and Groot bust a move, spot these spacecraft gadgets:

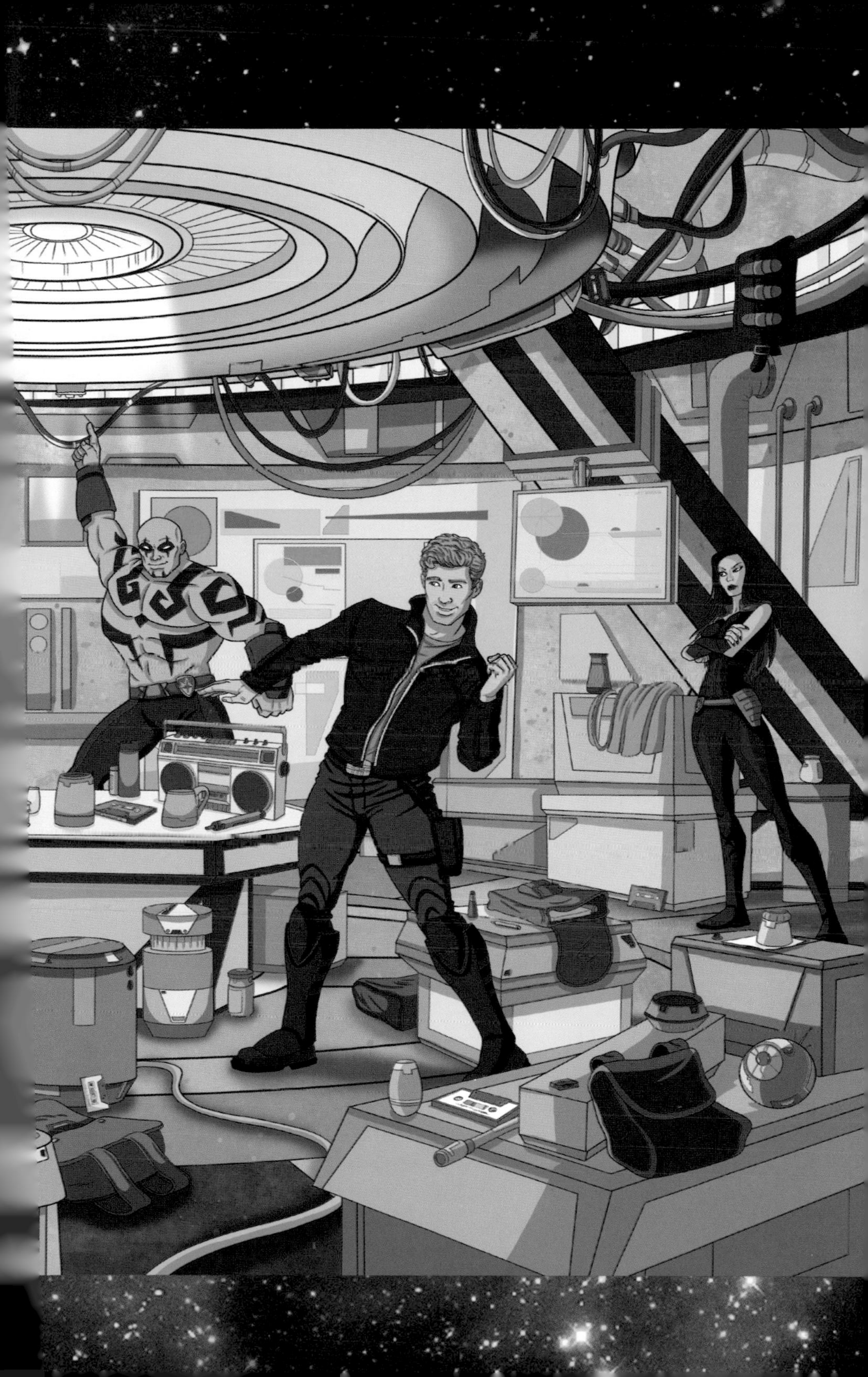

Zoom back to Xandar and look for these concerned citizens:

Dig and drill your way back to Knowhere and pinpoint 10 mining pods.

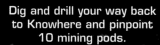
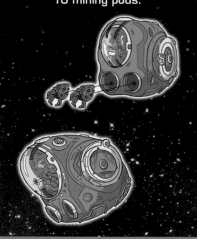

Bump back to Planet Pinball and spot these playful components:

BONUS

I AM GROOT

100

50

Plumb the depths of Pod H-2627 to find these strange species:

Groot has always appreciated the beauty of nature. Make your wooden way back to Planet X and uncover these fascinating floral features:

Return to Yondu Udonta's space scavengers while avoiding these aerial asteroids:

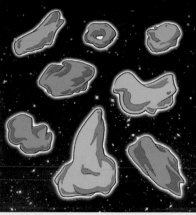

Rocket back to the *Milano*'s rescue mission and find these retreating Ravagers:

Peter Quill's collection is *almost* complete again! Boogie back to the *Milano* and find these additional mix tapes scattered around the ship:

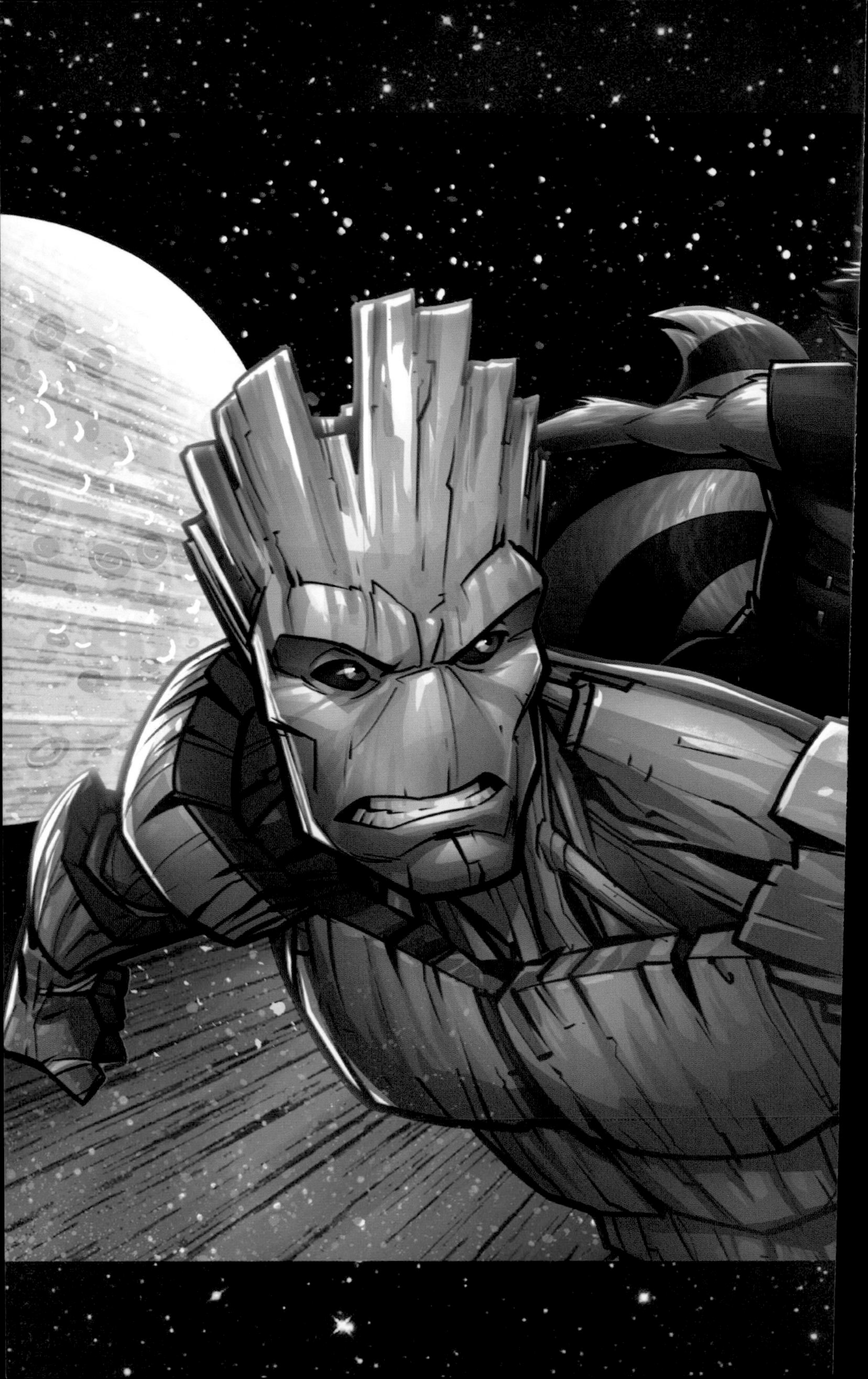